Hello
Lulu

To May
with love

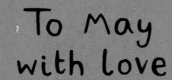

ORCHARD BOOKS
96 Leonard Street, London EC2A 4XD
Orchard Books Australia
14 Mars Road, Lane Cove, NSW 2066
1 84121 143 5
First published in Great Britain in 1999
Copyright © Caroline Uff 1999
The right of Caroline Uff to be identified as the author
and the illustrator of this work has been asserted by her in
accordance with the Copyright, Designs and Patents Act, 1988.
A CIP catalogue record for this book is available from the British Library.
1 3 5 7 9 10 8 6 4 2
Printed in Singapore

Hello Lulu

Caroline Uff

little ORCHARD

This is Lulu.

Hello
Lulu.

This is Lulu's house. "Come in!" says Lulu.

This is Lulu's car.

Brrmm Brrmm!

This is Lulu's Mummy

This is Lulu's baby brother.

He can say Lu-lu lu-lu.

This is Lulu's big sister. She goes to big school.

This is Lulu's Teddy.

One of his ears is a bit wobbly.

Lulu kisses
him better.

Look at Lulu's new shoes!

Red is Lulu's favourite colour.

Lulu's dog likes biscuits.

This is Lulu's Granny.

Lulu likes teatime at Granny's house.

But best of all
Lulu loves her family
and they all love her.

Bye bye
Lulu!